Sidney the Squirrel

www.traceythomson.com

First published
in 2019

ISBN:
9781090955869

Sidney the Squirrel

Stories with children's wellbeing at heart

Sidney the squirrel
wakes up one fine day

He jumps out of bed thinking
"What shall I play?"

At the back of his mind
is the thought of a chore

Something really important
but… oh such a bore!

He should gather some nuts
for the cold months ahead

But why bother?
Today he can have fun instead!

He can play hide and seek
with the birds
and the bees

Play tag
with a
dormouse

or simply
climb
trees

Deep down Sidney knows
there is work to be done

He should gather some nuts first
and then go
have fun

But he gets so distracted
his thoughts race so fast

It's tricky for Sidney to finish a task

His friends always tell him

"Slow down if you can"

"Cold weather is coming,
you really should plan"

"Gather some berries,
some nuts and
some seed"

"When there's snow
on the ground
you will need
things to eat"

So together they work
and they make a good start

But Sid soon gets distracted,
he stamps his foot hard!

"ENOUGH!"
shouts young Sidney

"I hear what
you say!

But there's still
lots of time so
today I will play"

A few weeks pass by
it grows colder each day

But Sidney the Squirrel
still just wants to play

He thinks about fetching
a fine nut or two

But there's always
exciting and fun
things to do

With places to visit
and new things to see

Sidney rushes around
feeling happy and free

He starts doing one thing
then finds a new game

He just can't stand still
it is always the same

Sid gathers up sticks
as he runs all around

Then he climbs up a tree...
up, up, high above ground

His friends down below
can hear banging
and noise

Sometimes Sid
sings songs
at the top
of his voice

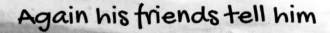

Again his friends tell him

"Come with us, don't play"

"Cold weather is coming,
no time to delay"

"Gather some berries,
some nuts and some seed"

"When there's snow on the ground
you will need things
to eat"

Now everyone thinks
 Sid's just messing around

 What no one can see
  from below on the ground

Is that Sid has a reason
to climb up, up high

He is building
a play house
way up in
the sky

Sid's hands can work wonders
he lets his thoughts race

Imagination set free
in his own special place

He can build and design
he just loves to create

A magical place
where he goes to escape

With his play house now built Sid says

"Come up and see
what I've made for us all,
you can come play with me!"

All his friends bring him gifts
when they come up to play

Now his cupboards are full
he gets more food each day

"Sidney the Squirrel can't focus"
they'd say

"He'll never succeed"
they looked on in dismay

But his mind
works in ways
they just don't understand

And look
what he's made...
It's the best in the land!

In exchange for some nuts
and some berries and seed

Sid's friends have a happy
and fun place to meet

When winter arrives
and snow falls on the ground

Sid is ready and able
and ever so proud

With help from his friends
he has found his own way

To get the job done...
and there's still time to play!

Printed in Great Britain
by Amazon

82346419R00020